RUBY'S HOPE
BY HANNAH TAYLOR

PUBLISHED BY The Ladybug Foundation Education Program Inc.

"This book is dedicated to the homeless and hungry of our world, who courageously do everything they can just to live until tomorrow. They are heroes in my heart."

HANNAH

ILLUSTRATED BY DON MONKMAN

Published by The Ladybug Foundation Education Program Inc.

Text copyright © 2006 Hannah Taylor

Illustrations copyright © 2007 The Ladybug Foundation Education Program Inc.

Edited by Tory McNally

Design by Doowah Design

Back cover photo by Joel Ross Photography

Printed in Canada by Friesens Corporation

For information, contact:
Director, The Ladybug Foundation Education Program Inc.
P.O. Box 21054,
Winnipeg Manitoba R3R 3R2

Visit our Website at www.ladybugfoundation.ca

Taylor, Hannah, 1996-
    Ruby's hope / by Hannah Taylor ; illustrated by Don Monkman.

ISBN 978-0-9784696-1-0 (bound).--ISBN 978-0-9784696-0-3 (pbk.)

    1. Ladybugs--Juvenile fiction. 2. Benevolence--Juvenile fiction.
I. Monkman, Don II. Ladybug Foundation Education Program III. Title.
PS8639.A949R82 2007   jC813'.6   C2007-906273-3

Once there was a little ladybug, how wonderfully happy was she.

e had a house, a family, and her
st friend, Bonnie Bumblebee. Oh
s, Ruby was a very lucky ladybug!

One day something different happened.

On her way to school, she was talking with every buggy on the bus when looking out from the window what did she see?

Why, it was a bumblebee just like her friend Bonnie!

But this bee was just sitting with her arms fully stretched,
asking for someone to help.

This bee wasn't like her friend Bonnie at all. This bug was in an old, worn, dirty,
beige jacket. Her hat just lay on the ground with a little bit of change in it.

 3

But aside from all that, the first thing Ruby did notice were the bumblebee's eyes. They were simply the saddest that she ever had seen. The tears in her eyes were bigger than the dew in the morning upon the leaves.

But just as they passed their eyes met, and Ruby felt something she'd never felt yet… Ruby felt terribly sad and quite angry.

Ruby wasn't angry at the bug on the street, but she felt most angry that the bug had to ask others for help. She was sad for the bug even though she didn't quite understand fully.

All through the school day, all Ruby could do was think of the bug she saw on the street.

Even at gym, when they played her favourite Basket Bug Ball!

Then later that night when Ruby climbed into bugbed, she asked her mom, "Momma, this morning I saw a bug on the street asking for food. Why does she do that?"

"Well," Mrs. Dotty hesitated. She was not excited about telling her 5 year old daughter about homelessness, but Ruby just had to know. "There are some bugs that are not as lucky as we are. Some bugs don't have a place to sleep tonight, a fridge to go to, and no buggy who loves them."

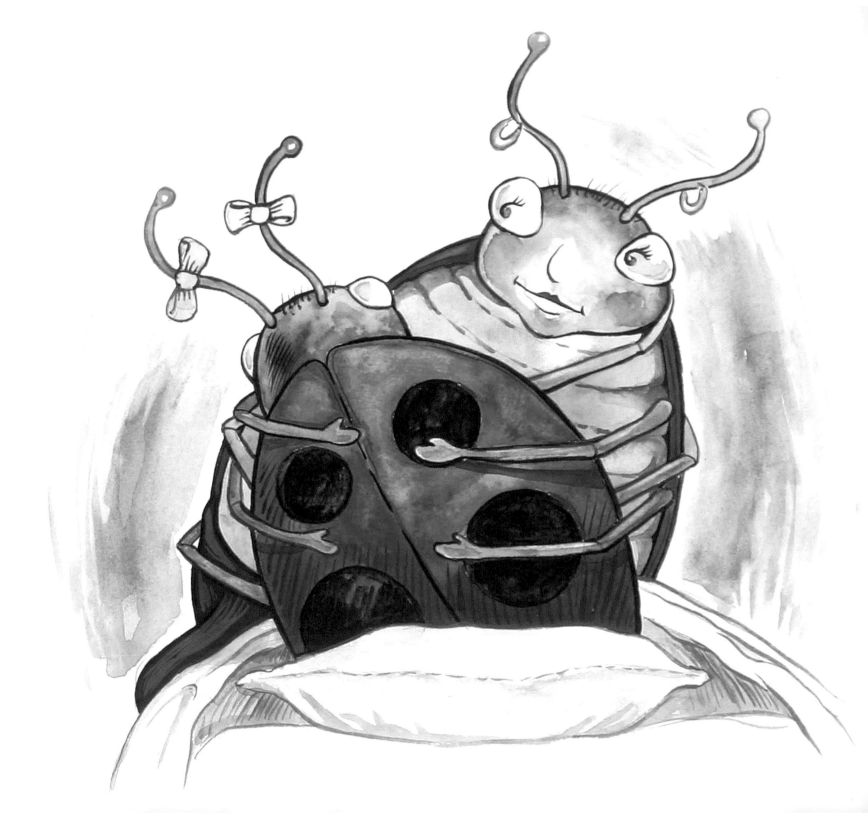

Ruby was silent for a few moments, then she said,
"It makes me awfully sad."

Momma replied, "Well, you know Ruby, if you do something to
help change the problem, your heart won't feel so sad."

There were a few seconds of silence.

"Good night Momma, I love you."
"Love you too," Momma replied. She turned out
the lights and Ruby went right to sleep.

As Ruby drifted off, she had a dream. She was flying high above Buggyville and she could see all the bugs who had no home. Some were cold! Some were hungry! All of them needed someone to help them! As she flew over they each looked at her with sad eyes as if to ask for help.

Ruby knew she had to do something.

Then she thought, "If every buggy is going to have a place to stay and food to eat we ALL need to care and help each other." She could then see all of Buggyville caring and helping each other, even the homeless bugs. With this wonderful thought dancing in her little head she woke up… it was time for school.

The next morning at Ruby's school, she went to her grade one teacher, Mrs. Hilderbug, and said, "Excuse me, I was on the bus yesterday morning and I saw a homeless bug on the sidewalk and it makes my heart feel really sad.

I want to do something about it. So I was wondering if I could talk to the class about homelessness, and have a lunch meeting with you to talk about what we could do to help."

"Why yes, of course, Ruby, that's the finest idea I've heard in a while."

Ruby's heart felt a little better.

So over buglunch, Ruby and Mrs. Hilderbug talked about Ruby's plan. Ruby spoke from her little sad heart. She believed if other bugs heard about the terribly sad-hearted bugs that lived a hungry and homeless life everyday that they would want to help and to care.

So off she did go with her plan in her mind and hope in her heart.

She stood in front of her grade one class and this is how her plan to help started. After hearing about homeless bugs on the street, her friends went to their parents and told them what Ruby had told them – that there were homeless, sad bugs who slept and lived out on the streets.

So all of the buggies, and their parents, brought to Bugmoral Hall school, buggie berrie pie, Nectar juice, and cozy bug blankets, to give to the poor. Her classmates drew their best pictures and sold them to all the big bugs who came out to help. Ruby's heart sparkled, her sadness disappeared, and her hope in the bugs that were now helping and caring grew.

Then Ruby noticed that as the bugs started to care for the homeless and hungry bugs, they also started to take better care of each other and the love really showed.

Ruby then realized even though she was just one little bug, if she tried with all her might and believed, she could show people that kindness, caring and sharing can change the whole world!

he great wonderful thing about giving love away is that you get a lot more love
1 return! So Ruby carried on with a heart full of love, wings dusted with hope,
and knowing that kindness can and will change the world.

Oh yes! Ruby was a **very** lucky ladybug!

About the Publisher

The Ladybug Foundation
Education Program Inc.

Hannah Taylor has founded two non-profit charities. The first, The Ladybug Foundation Inc., raises awareness and funds for the homeless and hungry in Canada. The second, The Ladybug Foundation Education Program Inc., is a separate charity that has conceived and developed "Make Change", a K-12 educational resource that creatively and passionately empowers children to get involved and make a difference in their world, at any age. "Make Change" is derived from the experience and example of Hannah and The Ladybug Foundation, to bring to life Hannah's simple message of caring, sharing and empowerment.

Learn more about The Ladybug Foundation and "Make Change": The Ladybug Foundation Education Program, at **www.ladybugfoundation.ca**

Proceeds from Ruby's Hope will help support The Ladybug Foundation Education Program Inc.